JAN 2 '11

YA
Fiction

Tonemah, P—

Animals.

THE ANIMALS TALK

Paula McGaa Tonemah
with Ed McGaa

ISBN: 978-1-57579-373-3

Library of Congress Control Number: 2009922531

Cover by Paula Tonemah

Edited by Crystal Dozier

Printed in the United States of America

PINE HILL PRESS
4000 West 57th Street
Sioux Falls, SD 57106

To my better half for his patience,
understanding and support – Larry White Bird

To my brother's memory – Daniel Lance Yellow Hand

To my wonderful granddaughter Angela

CONTENTS

CHAPTER ONE

MORNING AT THE CREEK

The morning sun streamed through the room, dancing brightly on the snow covered windowsills as if announcing a new day. Lance pulled the brightly colored, handmade quilts up to his chin, thinking to him self how great it was that yesterday was the last day of school, and that the snow was finally melting. Spring had officially arrived. As he lay snuggled in bed, he thought about Spirit Horse and the animal friends he had become acquainted with this past summer. He wondered how they were all getting along during the harsh Nebraska winter months and longed to see them again. So many times he got in trouble at school for daydreaming yet he knew he could never tell anyone about what happened at Fort Robinson. No one would ever believe that he had talked to animals about Crazy Horse and Indian ways.

The secret in some ways had become a burden. He wanted to tell someone so bad he felt he would burst. Someday he would be able to tell the history and the lessons he was taught but he wasn't sure when or how. He talked to his horse Daisy about everything he was feeling in his heart. Daisy had not spoken a word since they had said goodbye to Spirit, but it was comforting to know that she fully understood everything he said. She always looked at him with deep concern in her dark brown eyes.

"Lance, are you up?" Mrs. Wheeling's voice echoed through the bedroom door. "I've got your favorite, fresh out of the oven."

Without answering her, Lance was on his feet and grabbing his robe and slippers. "Biscuits!" During the school year there had not been much time in the mornings. Lance felt he barely had enough time to do his chores and get to school before his teacher quit ringing the bell, let alone sit down and enjoy his favorite meal – biscuits and jam. His mouth was already watering as the smell of fresh baked biscuits began to fill the entire house.

The Wheeling house was a log cabin with three rooms, one bedroom for Lance's parents and one room for Lance. The kitchen and living area was one big room with a large stone fireplace where Mrs. Wheeling did most of the cooking. The kitchen had a washboard and a cast iron oven that was fueled by wood. Just as Major Wheeling had promised last summer, there were two glass windows in the living area and one in each bedroom. Above the living area was a loft or company room as Mrs. Wheeling called it. In the loft she stored extra blankets and clothes and there was a puffy feather bed and chest of drawers for when company came to visit.

Lance poured a glass of warm milk and sat down at the kitchen table. "So, what are your big plans for today son? This is the first day of school vacation." Lance's father looked at Lance with a wide grin.

"I think I'll take Daisy for a long ride. I'm thinking about going up by the creek and see how much the ice has melted. I know that the trout will be running soon and I think trout for supper sounds just fine." Laughter filled the room. "What?" Puzzled, Lance looked at his parents. Major Wheeling laughed. "It's just the way you said that son, made it sound funny." As Major Wheeling laughed, it reminded Lance of White Crow laughing at Comanche when that silly horse was rolling on his back in the dirt. Once again Lance began to re-live those few brief days with his new found friends.

Lost in thought Lance quietly ate his biscuits. It was almost like he could see White Crow and the animals sitting in front of him. He counted each one of them. Looks Long the eagle, Stands Tall the bear with her granddaughter, Seeker the owl, Little Feet the wolf, Wanderer the deer, Grandfather, the buffalo and Starlight the mountain lion. He could hear the voices of Comanche and Spirit in his mind and he reached for the medicine bag he still wore around his neck. A cast iron pot banging near the fireplace snapped Lance's attention back to the kitchen. Lance realized that his father was staring at him. "Are you OK, son?" He asked. Mrs. Wheeling looked at her husband with a worried look. "Yeah Pa, I guess I was just daydreaming again. Boy, am I full! Guess I'll get dressed now. Thanks Ma for the biscuits."

Mrs. Wheeling's worried look turned to anger. "I don't know what happened when he went to visit you at Fort Robinson, but ever since he came back it's like he's in another world. In some ways he grew up a lot in those few days but in other…"

"I know," Major Wheeling interrupted her. "I know, it's like he's different somehow and always has his mind on something else. Maybe it's just a stage he's going through. He *will* be 14 soon." Mrs. Wheeling shook her head and went back to washing dishes.

Lance dressed in a hurry, eager to be outside and alone with his thoughts. He made sure he had on warm clothes and heavy socks. Grabbing his coat and hat he headed out the door towards the barn. The air was crisp and cool, but the sun added a hint of warmth. Daisy greeted him with a nod of her head. "No school today, Daisy. We're going to head up to the creek and see if it's melted any. Maybe we can do some fishing. It may get really warm this afternoon." Lance made sure Daisy's saddle was snug and secure. Placing his foot in the stirrup he pulled himself up on her back.

"Let's ride girl and see what the Creator will show us today." Daisy turned her head to look at Lance. She seemed to smile. Ever since Lance had listened to the lessons of the animals, he talked differently when he was alone with Daisy. His love for Grandmother Earth was becoming stronger, and so was he.

It was a peaceful ride. Patches of melting snow covered the prairie, tender grass shoots were beginning to appear; the trees sparkled with water droplets, everything smelled clean and fresh. Fallen leaves left a musty smell that mixed with the wet dirt. Lance took a deep breath. "Smell that Daisy? That's the smell of spring. It's just like White Crow told us. The white giant comes out of the north and covers Mother Earth leaving everything clean and new for the spring." Daisy kept plodding along at a slow pace but Lance knew she was thinking about what he said.

Lance looked above him and watched the clouds drift by. They looked like giant white fluffy birds in a sea of blue. Lance felt totally at peace. During the school year all Lance could think about was this moment, being able to take Daisy and go off somewhere in hopes of seeing his animal friends again. Lance thought about Comanche. "I wonder how many parades he has been in? He sure was a good friend, sometimes a bit silly, but a good friend." Lance always chuckled to himself when he thought about Comanche. "What a horse! To be able to survive the Battle of the Little Big Horn was something to be proud of. Comanche was indeed a true warrior."

Almost an hour had gone by when the creek finally came with in sight. Lance slid off Daisy's back and started walking towards the bank. Some ice still remained but you could see the water running freely. A brown trout lazily swam by and into a wide pool. "All right, I knew today would be a good day to do a little fishing! I hope you're hungry." Lance shook his finger at the trout.

Lance began unpacking his fishing gear that Daisy had been carrying. When everything had been unpacked, he decided that it would be nice to have a small fire. Not only would the fire keep him warm as he fished but he could also cook a fish for lunch. "Daisy, there's a small wood line just down the creek. I'm going to gather some wood for a fire. I'll be right back so don't run off."

The small grove of trees was good place for firewood with all sizes of dead wood lying on the ground. Lance began picking up the small sticks for kindling when heard a strange sound. He froze not sure what could be making the sound or what the sound was. He stood up straight and looked around but nothing was in sight. The sound made him very nervous so he moved quickly. After gathering up enough wood for his small fire, he hurried back to where Daisy was waiting. Still feeling a little frightened, he dropped the wood on the ground and began to build a fire. "Daisy, we'd better be careful. I heard a really strange sound but I didn't see anything." Lance stared at Daisy. He knew that horses could sense danger, but she didn't seem the least bit concerned.

It took a few minutes to get the fire going since the wood was still damp from the winter snows.

After the fire had burned a little bit it turned into a nice red and orange glow. Lance sat down and started to put his line, hook and bobber on his cane fishing pole. "There ya go. Now I can catch that big brown trout." Lance held up the fishing pole for Daisy to see. It took only a minute for Lance to catch his first fish. "There's lunch. Now we need to catch a few for supper." Lance felt quite pleased with himself. The morning went by quickly and after catching six nice size trout, Lance began to prepare one for his lunch. "Daisy, there is nothing better to eat than fresh spring trout. Hmmm hmmm!" Lance put the fish on a long stick and held it over the fire. "Daisy, you hear that? There's that noise again." Lance began to feel uneasy. "It almost sounds like a cat purring." Lance turned his head to look behind him and felt a tug on the stick. Whirling his head back around him, he was suddenly eye to eye with a huge golden mountain lion. Lance sucked in his breath his heart beating hard.

"Oh, don't be such a scaredy cat!" The mountain lion giggled.

"STARLIGHT!" Lance dropped the stick and jumped towards her, throwing his arms around her huge neck. "I wish you didn't enjoy scaring me so much."

Starlight ignored what he said. "I *really* like fish and this looks like a *really* good one. When are you going to eat?" Starlight began licking her paws and her lips, her eyes never leaving the trout.

Lance was so excited to see her he barely heard what she said. "Whoa wait a minute! I'll cook you your own. This one is for my lunch." He picked up the stick and held the fish over the fire. Starlight looked at Lance for a few seconds then with her great strength pounced on top of him. "Ha, now you dropped this one so not only is it dirty – it's MINE." Giggling she grabbed the fish off the ground and began eating it. The big cat looked up with a grin, "I don't need mine cooked." Lance wanted to be angry but could not help but laugh. "OK, you win. I'll cook myself another one."

Lance wanted to ask Starlight a thousand questions but he felt he needed to be polite and wait until after they had eaten. Starlight smacked her lips and commented on how good the fish was. Daisy stood in the background watching the two enjoy their lunch. After she had finished eating her fish, Starlight walked to the creek and got a drink of water. Her big tail waving in the air like a flag. Prancing back to Lance she sat down and starting licking her paws.

"Pilamiya Kola (thank you friend) that was a good snack." She licked her lips and added, "Wahsteayaloh Hogan" (a good fish).

Lance smiled at her. He couldn't help but think she looked like an overgrown kitten. "How is everyone? Did they have a good winter? I think about all of you all the time."

"I know, so much, in fact, that you didn't do that well in school this year." Starlight had a serious look.

Lance looked down at the ground. "I know. I just can't seem to quit thinking about those days I spent with all of you. I long to learn more and it seems I never really fit in at school." Starlight's playful look turned somber. "Balance boy balance. Remember I told you that everything has a balance. Yes, we wanted you to never forget the lessons that you learned, but we wanted you to use those lessons in everyday life. It's OK to think about us and to miss us. Even though we only spent a few days together we are a part of you and always will be. But you must use balance in all things. Think about the lessons we taught you but quit daydreaming and pay attention to what you are doing. The lessons all fit together. I told you about balance – Looks Long told you about observation. You can't observe if you are not focused."

Lance looked at Starlight with a blank stare. "What does focus mean?"

"Pay attention – think about what you do. Quit letting your mind wander." Starlight seemed annoyed.

"OK, I get it." Lance tried to smile.

"Now, here's what going on. Its spring and we will all be gathering together to talk and visit. White Crow and his family wintered over at the Pine Ridge Agency. We want to visit them. It will soon be time for Sundance. Even though the Indians have been put on a reservation, we animals still honor the old ceremonies and we need White Crow's advice."

"So what am I suppose to do?" Lance felt the excitement run through him.

"Pay attention and focus. Listening about the ceremonies will help you better understand the great leaders of the Indian People. Remember you were told that Crazy Horse was a very spiritual man. So were the other great leaders. Indian History cannot be properly told without including Indian Spirituality." Starlight's voice was deep and serious. She had lost all signs of her kitten look.

"Are any of the great leaders still living?"

"Yes, one of them is – Red Cloud."

For a few moments the two were quiet. Lance knew that once again he would be able to learn about Indian history and ways that were as old as time. He felt excited, but not scared as he was the first time they met. He knew in his heart that his animal friends would let no harm come to him.

"Starlight, why do they call him Red Cloud? How did he get his name?"

"I am not sure if it is true but I was told that on the night he was born, which was September 20, 1822, a giant meteorite swept across the sky. It was so big that it lit up the whole night from Minnesota to South Dakota. This meteorite was seen at Fort Snelling in Minnesota and by tribes far out in the plains. Many winter counts record this event. Many say it filled the night like a Red Cloud."

Lance thought about what Starlight was telling him. "Red Cloud is a very honorable name." Lance hesitated. "What is a winter count?"

"It's one way Indians record their history. It is painted like symbols on a deer or buffalo hide." Starlight moved her paws as if she were painting.

"I would like to know more about Red Cloud."

"Yes, well, I thought you would, but I am not the one to talk to about Red Cloud. You need to talk to Looks Long. He knows Red Cloud quite well. You can talk to him when you see him. Now I must move along. Things to do." Starlight giggled her silly giggle and stretched her long legs in front of her, flexing her claws.

Lance was aware that Starlight's kitten look had returned. She rose and turned to walk off, flicking her tail as if to say goodbye. "Wait...! How will I know when the meeting is?"

"Little Feet will come find you." Starlight called back not turning around. "Don't forget your fish." Starlight disappeared as quickly as she came.

"Well Daisy, we might as well put out this fire and head back to the house." Lance thought about Starlight. "She sure is arrogant sometimes, isn't she?" Daisy looked at Lance and rolled her eyes.

Lance got water from the creek and poured it on the fire. He made sure that no embers were glowing. He cut a limber twig with his pocket knife from a willow tree and threaded it through the fish's mouth and gills and then tied the twig together to make a loop. Gathering his fishing pole and fish he jumped on Daisy's back. "Head for home girl, Ma will cook this fish for dinner. I hope she will cook some potatoes, too."

The ride home was uneventful. Lance whistled a tune as they rode along. He thought about what Starlight had said about balance and wondered what new lessons he would learn. He also thought about Red Cloud and yearned to know more about this great leader.

When Lance and Daisy arrived home his parents were outside chopping wood. He held up the stringer of fish for his mother to see. "Wow Lance, nice catch. What would you like me to cook with it? Let me guess a big skillet of fired potatoes and some corn bread." Lance laughed as he jumped to the ground and handed his mother the trout.

Walking into the kitchen he could smell apple pie. "Are we having company, Ma?"

"I got a letter from you Uncle Andrew in South Dakota. He and your cousin Amy will be coming to visit today. Now don't give me that look, Amy and you will have a good time together."

Lance thought about what Starlight had told him. Little Feet would be coming to tell him when the gathering was. He didn't need Amy in the way. With his Uncle Andrew and Amy both here it would be hard for him to sneak away to the gathering.

"I know, Ma. I'll find something for us to do."

"Thank you. Now back to these wonderful fish you caught. It looks like there's plenty here for all of us.

As Mrs. Wheeling talked about the dinner menu, Lance thought about what he could do to get rid of Amy. "I'm going to go help Pa with the chores outside until they get here." The back door slamming alerted Mrs. Wheeling that her son had left the room. Shaking her head, she busied herself with the chores. She felt she had too much to do to worry about what Lance was thinking right now.

CHAPTER TWO

COMPANY ARRIVES

Lance was stacking the wood he and his father had chopped when he saw the wooden buckboard in the distance. Uncle Andrew and Amy's heads were bobbing up and down from bouncing on the rough road. The ground was slightly damp so only a small dust cloud followed them. The two dark brown horses seemed to pull the buckboard with ease. "Great, just great, now I've got to figure out what to do with Amy." Lance muttered to himself. He brushed the sawdust from his pants and started walking towards the house.

"Ma, they're here, I see them coming down the road. It looks like they will be here in about five or ten minutes." Lance called through the door of the kitchen.

"Oh gosh, is everything ready? I do love having company but there is so much to do." Mrs. Wheeling was in the loft putting clean sheets and blankets on the big feather bed. "Lance, tell your father I need his help with a few things please."

"OK, but where is he? I just came from the woodshed and he wasn't there."

"Then look in the barn, that's the only other place he could be if he's not in the house!" Mrs. Wheeling's voice had a tone of impatience.

Lance headed out towards the barn just as his father was coming through the barn doors. He had a worried look and held his rifle. "What's wrong, Pa?" Lance did not like the looks of this.

"I thought I heard some noises in the barn. My horse was acting pretty restless as if he sensed something. Daisy is calm though." Lance's mind raced, had Little Feet arrived already? "Don't get shook, son. I think it was just that owl that has decided to take up residence in our barn." Major Wheeling pointed to the roof. "He won't hurt anything being in there. Now, it looks like our company has arrived." Lance looked up and saw the owl sitting on a board in the eaves of the roof. "Seeker!" Lance gasped. Turning to see if his father had heard him, Lance breathed a sigh of relief. His father was already half way to the house. Seeker opened his big yellow eyes and gave him a wink. Lance was so happy to see him that his eyes began to water.

Seeker looked down at Lance and cocked his head. "Not good to keep company waiting." Moving his feet up and down, Seeker puffed out his feathers and closed his eyes again. Lance just kept smiling. "OK Seeker, have a good rest." Lance felt as if he was running on air as he turned and headed for the house.

Uncle Andrew and Amy unloaded their things from the buckboard. Mrs. Wheeling was so glad to see her brother that she started to cry. "Oh Andrew, look at Amy! She's almost as tall as I am." Andrew just nodded his head. They exchanged hugs and greetings then headed into the house.

After Uncle Andrew and Amy had brought all of their belongings into the house they all sat down to eat. As the adults talked, Lance just sat and stared at Amy. She was beginning to look more like a young lady than a little girl. Amy was only two years younger than him. Lance never really paid much attention to Amy in the past, she was just his girl cousin, but now he realized that she didn't look anything at all like Uncle Andrew. Amy had tanned skin and long dark hair. Her eyes were brown surrounded by thick dark lashes. She was turning into a very pretty young lady. "She must look like her mother." Lance thought to himself. "I wish I could have known my Aunt Abigail."

"Quit staring at me!" Amy's shrill voice broke Lance's stare. "I…. I'm sorry you look different." He replied.

Amy glared at Lance. "What do you mean different?"

"All grown up or something, geesh!"

"Don't start arguing." Mrs. Wheeling snapped at both of them then went back to her conversation with Andrew.

The rest of the evening Lance avoided Amy wondering why she acted the way she did. After Amy had gone to bed Lance went to check on Daisy and see if Seeker was awake yet. As he was walking towards the barn his father called to him. "Lance, I need to talk to you a minute."

Lance stopped and turned towards Major Wheeling. "Lance, I realize Amy was a little short with you at dinner so I thought I might explain it to you. Uncle Andrew brought Amy out here to spend some time with us this summer. Amy hasn't been the same since her Ma died a few years ago. I know you don't remember your Aunt Abigail. She was a fine woman. You're right, Amy does look different. She looks just like her mother, dark hair and dark skin. Abigail was a proud Indian woman." Lance looked at his dad in disbelief. "Aunt Abigail was Indian?" Major Wheeling gave his son a half smile. "Yes, son, she was. That makes Amy what they call a half breed. The town they lived in never accepted the fact that your Uncle Andrew had married an Indian. After Abigail died they hounded Andrew to send his "Little Heathen" to the reservation or to boarding school. In some states it's against the law to marry an Indian so Andrew and Abigail's marriage was not really accepted by some folks. Andrew met Abigail when he was trapping furs and trading with the Indians. Abigail was the love of his life and he was proud as punch of Amy when she was born. When Andrew goes trapping he takes Amy with him now. He's afraid something will happen to her. I don't blame him I'd do the same but now Amy really doesn't have a home. They travel all spring and summer. That's really no way to raise a girl." Major Wheeling shook his head.

"Pa, how did Aunt Abigail die?" Lance hesitated as he asked the question.

"We never talk about how she died to your Uncle Andrew because he thinks it's his fault. There was a time when Indians would get blankets from government agents that had Small Pox virus in them. It was a horrible thing to do and many Indian people died because of it. Uncle

Andrew had been up in Canada doing some trapping and trading when someone decided to give a blanket like that to Abigail. Since Andrew did a lot of trading with a lot of people he's not sure who the culprit was. He only felt that if he hadn't gone off to Canada, Abigail would be alive today. It's a pure miracle that Amy did not die as well."

Lance stared at his father. His heart was so sad for Amy and Uncle Andrew that he didn't know what to say. "I'll be little more patient with her, Pa." Major Wheeling placed his hand on Lance's shoulder. "I knew you'd understand, son." Lance stood frozen as he watched his dad walk back to the house.

"You look sad." Seeker's voice was low and soft. His big yellow eyes stared down at Lance with empathy.

"Did you hear what Pa said about Amy? I don't understand why people are like that. How can you have so much hate in your heart for someone just because they are not the same as you?" Lance kicked the dirt and balled up his fists. "It just makes me so mad!"

Seeker remained silent as Lance talked about how angry he was and how he could fully understand why Amy was angry. Finally when Lance calmed down, Seeker flew to a spot that brought the two of them eye to eye. "Anger will eat you alive. It is like a sore that festers inside of you. Amy will one day reach a time in her life that she can turn the anger into something good."

He didn't completely understand what Seeker was talking about but he knew in his heart that he would understand some day. Lance had come to realize that not all of life's lessons were easy and that sometimes things take a long time to understand.

"Now let's sit down and visit with each other." Seeker had a glint in his large yellow eyes. "I flew here and have been living in this barn for about two days. Winter was not too bad for me. I have had plenty of mice and other good things to eat."

Lance's thoughts turned into curiosity about his friends. "Have you had a chance to visit anyone else?"

"Oh yes. Looks Long is doing well. He has been visiting his brother in the Badlands. Grandfather is very busy with the herd. Looks like a lot of new calves will be born this spring. Wanderer has no real news. He continues to, well, just wander. Stand Tall is still asleep for the winter I won't see her for another month. You already talked to Starlight. Oh yes, I guess I'm still not fully awake. Very exciting news! Little Feet and his wife are expecting a litter of pups any day now. That is why they sent me. Little Feet does not want to be too far away until after the pups are born." Seeker cocked his head sideways as if he were quite proud of himself for relaying all the news.

"New wolf pups! I bet Little Feet is so proud he is about to burst." Lance couldn't help but smile at the thought of Little Feet being a father. "I bet he'll make a fine father."

"This will be the first time for Little Feet to have young ones. He's a bit nervous." Seeker bobbed his head up and down and laughed.

"Starlight said something about going and visiting White Crow about some sort of dance and ceremonies. What was she talking about?"

"Since all the Lakota have been moved to reservations now, I doubt very seriously if there will be a Sundance. The missionaries are trying to put a stop to all the ceremonies. They feel that the Indians should go to church and the children should start going to what they call boarding schools. But I do know that we will be able to have a Sweat Lodge hidden in the woods somewhere."

"Boarding school, is that where they want to send Amy? What is a boarding school?" Lance had a deep concern in his voice.

"Well let's see, this is May, 1880, right?" Lance nodded his head." So it would have been last September. A man by the name of Richard Henry Pratt went down to the Rosebud Reservation to try and recruit thirty six students for the Carlisle School. Pratt was an officer in the 10th Calvary. He led a group of Buffalo soldiers and Indian scouts at Fort Sill, Oklahoma. He really didn't trust the Bureau of Indian Affairs and he thought if he developed his own boarding school things would be better for the Indian children."

"But he was wrong, I take it." Lance had a bitter look on his face.

"True, but he did not know that at the time. In the middle of last year Pratt was given permission by the Secretary of Interior, Carl Schurz, and the Secretary of the War Department, McCary, to use a deserted military base for his school. Carlisle, Pennsylvania was chosen. So like I said, last September Pratt, and a teacher by the name of Miss Mathe, traveled to the Rosebud Reservation to talk to Spotted Tail, Milk and Two Strike. Miss Mathe was a former teacher at Saint Augustine and felt she could help the cause. She also speaks Lakota."

"Did they agree with her?"

Seeker shook his fluffy head. "No, not at first, they were not sure this would be good for the children. Pratt argued that with the government wanting all sorts of treaties signed it would be in their best interest for the children to learn to read English. The youngsters could interpret the treaties for the chiefs."

Seeker took a deep breath and sighed. There was a slight sadness in his eyes. "I have told you to always seek truth, Lance, but sometimes the truth isn't pretty. I have a feeling inside my heart that the boarding schools are not going to be a good thing for Indian children of any tribe."

Lance nodded his head. The children would be far away from their families.

"Spotted Tail and the others finally agreed to send some of their children. Happy with this, Pratt and Miss Mathe traveled over to the Pine Ridge Reservation to talk to Red Cloud and his people. Since Spotted Tail had agreed to send some children, so did Red Cloud. Red Cloud sent his grandson, and other leaders such as American Horse and Young Man Afraid of His Horses also sent their children. All in all, there were eighty two children that went to Carlisle School."

"Why do you think this is not a good thing?" Lance's curiosity was overpowering.

Seeker's big yellow eyes narrowed. "The children arrived in the middle of the night. They were tired, hungry and scared. They found no food, beds or anything that they needed. The children slept on blankets on the cold wet floor. The next day they were given uniforms and shoes. They were told that they could not wear the clothes they brought and they could not speak their native language anymore." Lance sucked in his breath. "Then the children had their hair cut! Many cried through the night. You do not cut the hair of a Lakota except when in mourning. The school called this act assimilation. The children were told that they no longer allowed to dress or talk like Indians anymore."

Lance could not believe what he was hearing. Those poor kids, kids his age being treated that way. All Lance could think about was that he did not want this to happen to Amy. There had to be someway that she could escape this. All thoughts of her being in his way this summer disappeared. Lance decided right then and there that he would do whatever he could to keep her around, at least for the summer.

A flicker in Seeker's eyes made Lance turn around and look behind him. Standing by the back door his dad held a kerosene lantern. Its light gave an eerie yellow glow. "Lance, are you OK? It's getting late, son. Time to go to bed, hurry and get the horses fed and come on."

"OK, Pa." Lance began to scramble around the barn. "Well Seeker, you're awake and I need to go to bed. I guess we'll talk more tomorrow about all this. It's a lot to think about."

"Truth can be hard to swallow sometimes. Speaking of swallowing I'm a little hungry. You sleep well my friend. I'm going to go find some breakfast." Silently, as owls are known for, Seeker flew out the door. Lance gave Daisy a pat on the nose then turned and walked to the house, muttering to him self about the evening's conversation.

Lance opened and closed the back door as quietly as he could. He knew that the door had a tendency to stick and he didn't want to wake anyone by slamming it shut. Standing in the kitchen with a mouth full of pie, Major Wheeling grinned at Lance. "Want a little snack before you retire, son?"

Lance couldn't help but laugh. "No, Pa. I think I'll just go on to bed. It's been a long day." Walking towards his room Lance stopped and looked towards the loft where Amy was sleeping. "We'll figure out something Amy. Just you wait and see." Lance whispered hoping that maybe some magic could happen with his words.

Sioux boys as they were dressed on arrival at the Carlisle Indian School, Pennsylvania. Photographed by J.N. Choate, October 5, 1879.

CHAPTER THREE
AMY'S NEW FRIENDS

The morning sun rose and so did the Wheeling family and their guests. Breakfast and morning chores were the main concern in Lance's mind. Lance lazily walked to the barn to feed Daisy and say good morning to Seeker. He always liked to check on Daisy first thing before breakfast. Seeker was still awake and seemed a little fatter than the night before. "Did you find a good dinner?" Lance looked up in the barn rafters. "Yes, as a matter of fact I did. Field mice are always my favorite. However I did manage to find a very delicious skunk." Lance looked at Seeker with disbelief. "A SKUNK, YUK!" Lance felt himself begin to gag. Seeker began to laugh a very hoot filled laugh. "We owls love a young skunk – quite a delicacy." Lance shook his head and held his stomach as he looked at Daisy. "Boy, I am glad you're a horse. After hearing about a skunk dinner I'm not so sure I'm hungry for breakfast anymore." Lance wasn't sure, but he thought Daisy was laughing at him, too.

It didn't take Lance long to finish his chores in the barn. Just as he was putting away Daisy's water bucket he heard a slight rustling sound which made him jump. "Who were you talking to?" Amy had a smug look on her face. Her long skirt had made the rustling sound as she entered the barn. "Or are you one of those crazy people that talk to themselves?" Lance wanted to say something ugly to Amy, but he thought about what his father had said and his promise to be more patient with her. "Just crazy, I guess." Amy turned and headed towards the house then stopped and looked back at Lance. "Auntie said breakfast is ready, so you better come on."

As Lance set down to breakfast Amy still had that smug look on her face as if she knew something he didn't. He wondered how much of his conversation with Seeker she had heard. It was hard to ignore her since her smug look was beginning to turn into a smirk. Lance made small talk through breakfast, and was just about finished when his father leaned back in his chair. "Well, what adventures are the two of you up to today?" Lance didn't quite know what to say. He had thought about going back to the creek and doing a little more fishing and hopefully visiting with Starlight again. He also wanted to talk more with Seeker. Doing anything with Amy was the furthest thing from his mind. He quickly tried to think of something to do that she would not enjoy.

"First off I think I'll brush Daisy real good. She's looking a little shabby."

Major Wheeling looked at Lance with a look only a father could give. He knew exactly what Lance was thinking. "That doesn't sound like much fun, son. I think you need to find something to do that both you and Amy can enjoy. After all, school is out now."

"OK, Pa." Lance was not pleased and still felt the sting of his father's glare.

"Now the two of you can help Mrs. Wheeling clean up the kitchen, then off you go. I want to see the two of you start your school break off right. Find something fun to do." Major Wheeling looked straight at Lance as he said this. Lance felt he was looking right through him. Uncle Andrew also gave a hard look towards Amy. "I expect you to behave yourself young lady." Amy's smirk disappeared. "Yes, Pa." She was suddenly very humble.

Once the kitchen was cleaned and Amy and Lance had retreated outside, Mrs. Wheeling stood in front of Andrew and her husband with her hands on her hips giving them both an icy stare. "Now what was that all about? Those children will learn to get along just fine if the two of you will just stay out of it." Before either of the men could reply, she turned back towards the kitchen to finish her work.

Lance didn't really like Amy following him so closely. She seemed to be right on his heels. "Do you have to walk so close to me, and do you have to have that smirk on your face?"

"You're not going to brush your horse, you're going to talk to that owl some more." Amy's voice was shrill. Lance stopped dead in his tracks. "What are you talking about?" Amy stood and folded her arms. "That owl you were talking to – like he could talk back. Owls are stupid." By this time they were both standing in the doorway of the barn. Before Lance could even answer her Seeker flew down and landed on a post. "I beg your pardon, I am not stupid." Lance felt his heart beating hard as Amy let out an ear piercing shriek. Before he realized what he was doing Lance clasped one hand over Amy's mouth with the other hand he held her head so she couldn't move. "Hush, you'll give away the secret." Amy tried to pull away. "I'm not going to let you go until you promise me you won't scream." Amy nodded her head. "You must never tell anyone." Amy nodded her head up and down. Lance could see the fear in her eyes. Slowly he let go of her. "Promise?" Seeker cocked his head back and forth watching the two of them.

Amy stood dumbfounded staring at Seeker not knowing what to think or say. Seeker stared back, his big yellow eyes never blinking. "My, my you do look just like your mother." Amy's eyes began to fill with tears. "You knew my mother?" She forgot all about her fear or screaming again.

"Oh yes, she too was one that talked to us, and she talked a lot about you." Amy's tears turned to a smile. "It is good that you are here with Lance. Now you too can learn the history of your people. Now have a seat and let us visit." Seeker was not as polite as he usually was when he told her to sit down. Amy's fear gave her no choice but to obey.

Amy was still shaking as she silently sat down on a bale of hay. She listened intently as Lance and Seeker excitedly told her how they had met at Fort Robinson. Lance told her all about Tahshuunka Wakan (Spirit Horse) Comanche and all the others. Amy began to relax and enjoy the story. She smiled as he talked about White Crow and about Little Feet's good news. Lance felt that a huge burden had been lifted off his shoulders. He finally had someone that he could share his secret with. They laughed together as he told her about Starlight scaring him down at the creek.

The morning flew by as they talked and laughed. Amy's face had grown some softness about it and her anger seemed to fade. "Lance, look at Seeker." Amy pointed towards the rafters of the barn. Seeker had his feathers so puffed out that he looked as wide as he did tall. "Well, I guess we better let him sleep." Lance was trying not to laugh. Quietly the two slipped out of the barn and into the afternoon sunshine.

"Lance, do you really think Seeker knew my mother?"

"Of course, why else would he have said that? Seeker is named Seeker because it is his job to always seek the truth in everything. I'm sure he will be happy to share what he knows about her."

For the first time Lance was aware that Amy was smiling. Not just a pretend smile, but a real one as if she were really happy. "I miss her a lot." Amy looked up at the clear blue sky.

"I know you do, but things will get better. Hey, let's take Daisy up to the creek and see if we can find Starlight."

"YES!" Amy let out a silly giggle. Before they knew it, Daisy was saddled and ready to go. Amy and Lance jumped on her back and headed towards the creek. They enjoyed the ride. They talked about school and family and what they wanted to do when they grew up. Amy seemed to know a lot about the different plants that grew along the trail to the creek.

"Stop here, I want to show you something. My Ma taught me a lot about the herbs around here."

Lance pulled the reins to bring Daisy to a stop and Amy jumped off. "See this fuzzy green plant that's just now peeking its head through the ground? It's Mullein. If you take these leaves and put them in hot water you can make a tea. It's good if you have a bad cold, or you can use it if you have sprained ankle. Just soak your foot in it." Lance was just about to ask Amy a question when he heard a familiar screech in the sky. "Looks Long! He's here – look in the sky, Amy. See his pure white tail feathers?" Amy shielded her eyes with her hand then waved. Looks Long let out another screech to acknowledge her. "Let's get to the creek. That's where he's headed." Jumping on Daisy's back, Lance and Amy made a mad dash for the creek. Looks Long flew over head just slightly in front of them.

Amy and Lance watched as Looks Long circled lower and lower until he landed on a large rock by the creek. Lance could tell that Amy was impressed by how beautiful and large Looks Long was. Looks Long hopped down off the rock and began circling Amy, looking her up and down. "Don't worry, he did that to me the first time I met him. He likes to look at everything. That's why they call him Looks Long." Lance grinned as he remembered the first time he met Looks Long. Amy stood very still and very quiet while Looks Long circled her.

Looks Long stared deep into Amy's brown eyes. "Abigail was your Ina. She had a good heart, so do you."

"My Ina?" (eeh – nah) Amy was puzzled.

"Your mother – Ina means mother." Looks Long stretched his powerful wings. "She was a good woman. She too followed the ways of her people. She had a love for all animals and respected Old Grandmother Earth. So many things she taught you. More than you probably even realize.

All that she taught you will serve you well as you grow up. You have a proud heritage. Never forget that."

Amy felt sad thinking about her mother, but at the same time felt excited with the idea that she could learn more about her people. What a morning this had become. As she let her thoughts wander for a moment she was jolted back with the smell of fur and hot breath on her neck. She froze looking at Lance who seemed to have a silly grin on his face. Her mind raced as she turned to look into two very large yellow eyes. "Oh my gosh, you must be Starlight!" Starlight looked at Lance. "She doesn't scare as easy as you do, Lance. She'll be more fun." Lance rolled his eyes. He knew Starlight could not resist teasing him. Rolling on her back as if she were a big house cat, Starlight looked at Lance with kitten eyes. "I'm hungry. I want another fish." Starlight whined loudly. Amy started laughing and felt she would never stop. Lance just looked at Starlight thinking that she was probably the silliest thing he had ever seen, but he could not help laughing as well.

Amy and Starlight giggled and talked as Lance untied his fishing pole from Daisy. Looks Long sat quietly staring up into the clouds. After Lance sat down and threw his line in the water Looks Long began to speak. "I visited White Crow and his family yesterday. They are doing very well and told me to tell you that they think about you often. He gave me instructions on how to build a sweat lodge. We will build it tomorrow here at this creek. Then we will have an Inipi (sweat lodge ceremony). We will do it in the afternoon. You and Amy will learn much tomorrow. We will also pray for Amy since she has lost her Ina (mother)."

"I was hoping to get to see White Crow again." Lance could not hide his disappointment.

"It is too dangerous. All Indians have been ordered to stay on the reservation right now." Looks Long was also disappointed but tried not to show it.

"Who will build the Sweat Lodge?"

"The best builders on the earth!" Looks Long laughed. "The beavers."

Lance shook his head. "Why did I even ask?"

Looks Long and Lance talked about tomorrow's events as he fished. Before the afternoon was over, Lance had caught enough fish for everyone to have a nice lunch. Amy had built a small fire to cook the fish and had some cookies stashed in the pocket of her dress that she shared. They all agreed it was a fine meal. Looks Long preferred his fish raw, but did agree that the cooked fish smelled good. The afternoon sun was a welcome change from the chilly morning, and after eating such a nice meal, Starlight decided it was time for nap. She wandered off to find a comfortable place to sleep. Amy was also getting a little sleepy and suggested they head back to the house.

"Looks Long, I really wanted to ask you some questions about Red Cloud." Lance was not ready to leave. Looks Long stared at the sky again. "Tomorrow morning I have to give the beavers instructions. Come back in the morning and I will tell you what I know about Red Cloud." Lance started to argue but felt it would be disrespectful and just nodded.

Amy helped Lance put the fire out and tie the fishing pole back on to Daisy's saddle. Daisy looked ready to go, too. "Lance, I think the warm sunshine has made Daisy sleepy." Lance looked at Daisy's half closed eyes. "Well, it's probably good that we all get some rest. Sounds like tomorrow will be a busy day."

CHAPTER FOUR
BACK TO THE CREEK

Amy was so excited when she woke up she felt like she couldn't breathe. Running downstairs, she didn't even stop to say good morning to her father. Lance was already up and sitting at the kitchen table eating breakfast. Both of them grinned when they saw each other. They knew this would be a day to remember. "Is there any reason the two of you are grinning like cats that swallowed canaries?" Mrs. Wheeling teased. Before Lance could answer, Amy said quickly, "Its spring and the baby animals are out. I can't wait to go for a ride." Lance just nodded his head. He was surprised that Amy lied so quickly. The two gulped down their breakfast and headed out the door to get Daisy.

"What's going on? Those two are in a big hurry." Major Wheeling looked at Andrew with amazement. "These are the same two kids that didn't get along yesterday."

"I told you if you left them alone they'd be fine." Mrs. Wheeling's voice was smug.

Uncle Andrew sat down to the table. "I'm sure they're fine. Probably found some tadpoles in the creek or something. Breakfast sure looks good. Sit down and don't give it another thought. They're just being kids."

Outside, Amy and Lance hurried to get Daisy ready to go. Seeker watched from the loft as they scurried around the barn. "You might want to slow down a little bit. Everyone will be there when you arrive. No need to rush."

"Are you coming, Seeker?" Lance was really hoping he would join them.

"I will be there later. It's still too early in the day for me. Travel safe." Seeker closed his big yellow eyes and fluffed out his feathers. His sleepy voice told Amy and Lance that he was in need of a nap. "See ya later, Seeker." Lance called to the rafters as he and Amy rode out of the barn.

The ride to the creek seemed to take forever. The spring sun shone brightly and there was not a cloud in the sky. Amy and Lance agreed that it couldn't be a more perfect day. As they came near the creek they could see the beavers running back and forth. Looks Long was perched in a pine tree on a lower branch, his keen eyes taking in every detail. Starlight was stretched out on a grassy spot sunning her self. If you looked closely you could see a slight twitching of her tail. She did not seem the least bit concerned with the activity around her.

Amy watched for a moment then turned to Lance. "How do they know what each other is saying? I don't understand."

"Comanche told me that animals have no language problems, they understand each other and all human languages as well. It's just the way the Creator made them; it's only humans that don't understand each other." Lance's voice had a serious tone. Amy looked at Lance then towards the beavers. "Well, that makes sense."

Looks Long called out to Lance, "Hau Kola" (hello friend). As Lance walked over to stand near Looks Long, Amy sat down on a rock close to Starlight. Starlight opened her eyes slightly and gave Amy a wink. "The beavers are doing a fine job, Lance. They have cut down enough willows to build the sweat lodge and enough firewood to heat the stones that will go inside." Looks Long could tell that once again Lance had a hundred questions. "I will explain things as the day goes by, but now it is time for a break from our work." Looks Long used his beak to point towards the beavers. In single file they dove into the water. Each beaver glided across the water silently, their dark brown fur glistening in the morning sun. Two of the beavers flipped on their backs and floated like clouds in a summer sky.

"I wish I could swim like they do. They are so graceful, but so powerful." Looks Long had a misty look in his eyes. Lance's laughter made Looks Long spin his head around. His misty look turned to irritation. "What's so funny about that?"

"I'm sorry. It's just that the thought of you swimming seems so silly. You have legs but you don't have any arms – you have wings!" Lance tried to quit laughing.

"Haven't you ever dreamed of being able to fly? You don't have wings, nor do you have feathers." Looks Long's voice was almost angry.

Lance sucked in his breath feeling a little embarrassed. He had dreamed about being able to fly. Suddenly he realized that his dream of being able to fly might look silly to an eagle. "The Creator has given all of us certain abilities, Lance, and it's all right to dream of being able to do things like fly or swim, but we should never laugh at someone for using their imagination or make fun of their hopes and dreams. You never know if those dreams might turn into reality."

"Yes, sir." Lance's voice was soft.

"Think about it. Who knows, someday someone might build something that will allow humans to fly." Looks Long laughed at his own words. "Allow humans to fly! Ha!"

The two sat and laughed about this and talked about how it could be possible. Their laughter was stopped by Amy's voice. "Look, oh my gosh, look!"

Lance and Looks Long turned to look behind them to see what Amy was pointing to. Coming through the trees with the rustling of leaves was Spirit carrying White Crow on his back. Lance felt that his heart was going to explode. The two looked so majestic. Spirit's white and brown mane blew gently in the breeze as he walked towards them. White Crow sat very straight and tall on Spirit's back, the sunlight glistening off the beautiful beadwork sewn on his buckskin shirt. White Crow climbed off Spirit's back and shook Lance's hand. "It is good to see you again." Lance wheeled back. "I understand you." He looked at Amy. "Before I could not understand what White Crow was saying without holding on to Spirit's ear." He turned back to White Crow. "I'm sorry – it is so good to see you. I was afraid I would never see you again."

Starlight's voice echoed behind them. "Today we will all understand each other's language. You and Amy will be allowed use the animal's gift of understanding."

"But only for today, Lance." Spirit's voice brought back a wonderful feeling for Lance. "After today things will go back as they were. White Crow is here to lead the sweat lodge and teach you and Amy a song. Grandfather Buffalo has also sent buffalo hides that we will put over the sweat lodge now that the beavers have finished cutting the willows for the frame."

"Spirit, White Crow, this is my cousin Amy. She is staying with us this summer." Lance almost forgot his manners.

Spirit walked up to Amy and looked her up and down. "I'm sure you have heard this many times. You look just like your mother. You have your mother's spirit as well. I'm glad that you are here." Amy gingerly reached her hand out to Spirit. He lowered his head and let her stroke his nose. His soft eyes gave Amy a feeling of peace. A feeling she had not felt since her mother had died.

"Pylamia Tashuunka Wakan." (thank you horse) Amy continued to stroke Spirit's nose.

"How much of your language do you know?" Spirit's voice had a hint of surprise.

"I have forgotten a lot of words. My dad helps me practice, but with no one to speak my language with I am starting to forget. With all the talk of sending me to boarding school I sometimes don't practice like I should. I heard that we are not allowed to speak our language there."

Starlight gave a low growl. The type of growl that would make you skin crawl. White Crow was walking towards the sweat lodge area and froze in his tracks. "We have not heard good things about the boarding schools, but since you do not live on a reservation maybe there will be a way made for you so that you will not have to go."

"Don't give up hope, Amy." Lance smiled at her but inside he was worried. Looks Long broke the serious conversation. "Well, we can only handle what we have to do today, and today we shall pray to the Creator and show how we are grateful for our lives and for today."

"That's right, and today we must finish the sweat lodge." This was an unfamiliar voice. They all turned to see a very wet beaver and began to laugh. Beavers are known for their sense of humor. With his paws in the air and a silly grin the beaver addressed Amy. "My name is Cutter and this is my family. You must be Amy, and this young man with you must be Lance."

Amy tried not to look shocked. "Nice to meet you."

"Good morning Spirit, White Crow." Cutter nodded to each of them. Without warning, Cutter turned quickly and began rubbing his soaking wet fur against Starlight's side. "Ah, stop it!" She yelled. "You know I hate water, what's wrong with you?" Cutter started laughing so hard he fell over. "That's for all the times you snuck up and scared me." As Starlight stormed off she gave a hard whip to her tail towards Cutter. She wanted to quickly leave the laughter behind her.

"Don't go away too far Starlight," Cutter called out. "I will need you to help bend the saplings after I place them upright in a circle for the lodge."

The sweat lodge was beginning to take shape. Each of the willows was bent and fastened to the ground after a hole was dug. The hole was just big enough for the larger end to fit in. The beavers made the larger end of each willow pointed so it could more easily stick in the ground. The willow frame looked like a dome. Inside the dome the ground was leveled and a hole was dug in the middle. Looks Long explained that the hot rocks would go into the hole and that water would be poured over them to create steam. White Crow would also put sage on the rocks that would give off a sweet smell. The opening in the front would be where everyone would crawl in. After everyone was seated, they would sing and they would pray. The fire keeper would add more rocks and White Crow would add more water. Four times they would do this. The steam would make everyone sweat, and the sweat would be cleansing.

"How is the steam going to stay in?" Lance stared at the dome frame.

"That is why Grandfather sent the buffalo robes. We will place them over the dome. It will be very dark in there." Looks Long waited for Lance to ask more questions but he just kept staring at the frame.

Amy and White Crow had started a fire. As Spirit watched the fire, Cutter and his family began to put rocks in the fire to heat them. It was almost time to begin. Amy and Lance began to understand how sacred this ceremony is. Once the rocks were heated, White Crow lit some sage and everyone lined up. One by one they walked up to White Crow as he waved the smoke from the sage around them. As each entered the sweat lodge they said quietly "Mitakuye Oyasin" (we are all related) and crawled into the lodge. Once everyone was seated just like Looks Long had described, Cutter brought in hot rocks with the aid of a discarded elk's antler. White Crow poured water on the rocks and began the ceremony.

"I have a simple song that I want to teach you," White Crow stated. "I call it my appreciation song. We all should appreciate to the Great Spirit, Wakan Tanka, that we live." He then called on beaver to beat his tail against the soft earth which made a drum like sound.

"Wakan Tanka, Wakan Tanka," he called out. "Listen closely," he instructed, "because after I tell you this song you will all have to sing it."

"Wakan Tanka

Pilamiya

Wakan Tanka

Wichoni Heyy!" He sang out, his voice clear and strong.

"Wakan Tanka is the Great Spirit, The Maker, The Provider, and the All Powerful that looks over us. Pilamiya is thank you. Wichoni means that I live or that we all live." Cutter beat his tail against the soft ground and all began to sing, led by White Crow.

Lance felt that he had never heard anything more beautiful then the sounds of everyone singing. Four times they did this. Four times the door was opened, fresh air let in and four times Cutter brought heated rocks. Four times they prayed – four times for the four directions.

When the ceremony was over, Lance could not describe how he felt. He only knew that something had happened that made him feel that everything was good in the world. Later, Amy told him she finally felt a sense of belonging. She now understood what her mother had told her about spirituality. They both felt that their prayers had been heard.

Laughter filled the air as the beavers dived into the water again. Starlight had unpacked the food White Crow had brought and everyone began to eat and enjoy themselves. Lance knew that it was getting late in the afternoon, and soon he and Amy would have to leave.

"Looks Long, I know we have had a busy day, but I still would like to know more about Red Cloud." Lance wasn't sure if it was proper to ask at this time but his curiosity got the best of him.

"Red Cloud – Makhpia Lutah, he is a good man and a fine warrior." White Crow smiled.

"I know I promised you that we would talk today about him, but time has gotten away from us, Lance. Can you wait until tomorrow and my mind will be more on history?" Looks Long did look tired.

"I'm sure you're right. Tomorrow will be better. Amy and I need to get back soon so that my folks don't worry." Lance was disappointed but he understood. He was tired, too.

"A cool swim will refresh you and you won't stink!" The voice and the laughter could only be one animal. Lance looked up and saw Cutter casually floating on his back and eating a carrot at the same time.

"Well, I'm not going swimming with my clothes on." Amy quipped. "But, I will wash my face." She cupped her hands and splashed cool water in her face. "Lance, we do need to get back, Looks Long, what is left to do?"

Looks Long looked around but he didn't see any work left. Spirit had stomped out the fire. White Crow had packed up the buffalo robes and Starlight had given out any left over food to whoever wanted it. "I think we are finished here for today. We will leave the frame of the lodge where it stands. You children get back home, but come back here tomorrow to learn about Red Cloud." Looks Long sounded very much like the elder that he was becoming.

White Crow looked at Lance's sullen face and knew what he was thinking. "We will see each other again, don't worry." Lance smiled and shook White Crow's hand. Goodbyes were said to all. Amy hugged Starlight and kissed her on the nose. Starlight giggled, her kitten look had returned. She seemed to have forgiven Cutter for getting her wet and everyone laughing at her.

Lance, Amy, and Daisy got home just in time for supper. The rest of the evening was spent resting and visiting with each other. Early to bed and a good night's rest was the plan. Lance and Amy both drifted off to sleep quickly with thoughts of what tomorrow would bring.

CHAPTER FIVE

AN UNUSUAL HISTORIAN

Lance had fallen into a deep sleep. He was dreaming of everything that had happened that day, reliving every wonderful moment. Outside a storm was brewing, bringing with it lightning and rain. Lance awoke to the sound of thunder. As he gazed out his window, he could see the lightning dancing on the prairie. A shadow in the night sky grasped his attention. "Seeker ?" Lance wondered why he would be out in the storm. Landing on his window sill, Seekers yellow eyes were wide and bright. "Good news Lance – good news!" He fluffed his wet feathers. "Little Feet is now the proud father of two beautiful pups, a fine healthy girl and a strong handsome boy."

"Oh, that's wonderful. I'm sure he is really proud. I wish I could see them." Lance was so excited he was shaking. "Is that why you are out in this storm?'

"I had gone to check on Little Feet and his family. I just got here when the rain started. I have been flying as fast as I could to beat the storm. Whew!" Seeker was slightly out of breath. "I was hoping you would be awake so I could share the news. Now off to bed you go. I'm going to make myself comfortable in the barn." With one powerful swoop Seeker was gone.

Lance lay in bed listening to the rain that had begun to fall. The exciting news kept him from falling asleep right away. He would give anything to see Little Feet's new pups. He tried to imagine what they looked like and what they would named. Half way through his thoughts he began to drift off.

Amy and Lance were both feeling sad as they ate breakfast. There was a steady rain outside and they knew that they would not be able to go back to the creek. Mrs. Wheeling sensed their disappointment. "I'm sure the two of you can find something to do inside. Besides we need the rain for the garden." Amy and Lance looked at each other and shrugged their shoulders.

"What's the matter with you two this morning?" Uncle Andrew said in a teasing voice.

"We just wanted to be outside." Amy whined loudly.

"Well you could still go out in the barn. Neither one of you have done your chores the last few days." Mrs. Wheeling knew that wasn't what they wanted to hear, but she also knew it would keep them busy.

"Good morning, we sure need this rain." Major Wheeling sat down to the table as Mrs. Wheeling brought him some coffee. "Your mother is right, Lance. There are some chores in the barn you two need to do. By the time you're done the rain will probably stop and you can go back to the creek. You do know that after a rain is always a good time to go fishing." Major Wheeling gave his son a wide smile.

Lance and Amy looked around the barn as if they had never been there before. Seeker was sleeping comfortably in the rafters. The two said very little to each other as they did their work. They fed the horses and gave them fresh water. Amy brushed Daisy as Lance cleaned out the stall. Quietly they worked side by side. The rain had slowed down to a drizzle giving them hope it would soon end and the sun would come out. Occasionally they would look at each other and sigh.

"What a couple of gloomy gooses." An unfamiliar voice echoed across the barn.

"And just who are you?" Amy quipped with a sharp tone.

The eagle cocked his head back and forth looking Amy over. He was a young bald eagle yet looked quite large sitting on the horse stall door. "I'm Talks Right, Looks Long's brother. You must be Amy, and the boy with you is Lance."

Lance leaned on the rake he was holding. "Nice to meet you, are you the one who knows about Red Cloud?" Lance held his excitement.

"Yes, he is." Little Feet's voice made Lance jump with happiness. Little Feet you made it! Oh, I am so glad to see you! How are your children?" He threw his arms around Little Feet's neck.

"Yes, yes tell us about your pups!" Amy was dancing around the barn.

"They are fine and healthy. They look like their mother, just beautiful."

"What are their names?" Lance knew they would be fine names. We will name them at a naming ceremony soon, but in the meantime, Talks Right has come to tell you about Red Cloud." Little Feet pointed to Talks Right with his nose.

In all the excitement neither Amy nor Lance had noticed that Looks Long had flown in the barn and was sitting by his brother. The two eagles looked very elegant sitting next to each other. Lance and Amy sat down on a bale of hay both facing Talks Right to show him that he had their full attention.

"They call me Talks Right because I tell the truth about past events. As you know, we believe that the Creator is all truth. I try to be that way as well. I am a historian. In our culture history is passed down from generation to generation. We are not allowed to add a word or take away even one word, that way the history is accurate and not a story. The older historians practice the history with us until we have it memorized perfectly." Talks Right had lost his youthful voice and spoke in a serious tone like his brother, Looks Long.

Talks Right continued. "Starlight has already told you how he got his name. Red Cloud has many followers and it would take all day to tell you of his many victories in battle. He was only sixteen when he went out on his first war party, and it was then that he claimed his first scalp. Red Cloud is a big man and stands over six feet tall which is an advantage when you are in battle."

"Six feet tall, I've never seen anyone so tall!" Lance was embarrassed when he realized that he had spoken his thoughts out loud. Amy put her finger over her mouth and made a "shh" noise.

"Yes, he is a large man in height but also a large man inside." Talks Right continued. "Red Cloud soon became known as an excellent warrior and the people admired him."

Amy had a quizzical look. "Why did they admire him?"

"Many reasons – for instance in 1841 there were only a few wagon trains coming through this area headed west. One or two a year was all that was seen. Then gold was discovered in California and the wagon train count went from one or two a year to over 50,000 a year. The soldiers did whatever they could to try and keep the wagon trails open by offering the Indians presents and treaties. The soldiers wanted more and more settlers to peacefully come across the land. Yet they did not understand that Indians did not want the presents and treaties they were offered by the government, they wanted to freely hunt buffalo. Buffalo was becoming scarce and forts were continually being built along the Bozeman Trail. The forts replaced the trading posts. At one time the Indians enjoyed coming to the trading posts. It was a friendly time to trade and to see old friends. "

"That's the way I feel when Pa takes me into town in the summer. We buy things like flour and sugar and I always see some of my friends from school. Sometimes Pa buys me licorice sticks." Lance smiled at the thought of going into town.

"Lance, if you went into town thinking it was going to be fun and then find soldiers there instead of friends, wouldn't that make you mad?" Amy replied. "It would be like going to the garden to pick vegetables and finding rabbits. You know they are just doing their job, but you also know if you don't watch them they will destroy the garden."

"Exactly," Little Feet spoke up. "We have to think about our families and always be on the look out for enemies that might hurt them. As head of my pack I have to keep a watchful eye. Unfortunately we can not always trust others, especially when they have a history of doing us harm."

Talks Right agreed with everyone and continued. "Red Cloud made it known how all these settlers were affecting his people. He fought back until 1868 when he signed the Fort Laramie Treaty. With that treaty all the forts on the Bozeman Trail were shut down. Red Cloud was smart enough to **not** sign the treaty until all the forts were shut down and the troops gone. From 1866 through 1867 Red Cloud and his people fought hard. This time will always be known as Red Cloud's War."

Lance and Amy looked at each other with big grins. Talks Right took a deep breath. "Red Cloud accomplished many things for his people, not only signing the Fort Laramie Treaty but he collected horses, guns, and ammunition. This is what helped win the Battle of the Little Big Horn. It is said that he has over 80 coups, yet he recognized the talent of others, such as Crazy Horse."

Looks Long nodded his head. "Crazy Horse was a good choice."

"Yes, he was." Talks Right had sadness in his eyes as he thought about Crazy Horse. "Crazy Horse was only about 22 years of age when Red Cloud decided that he would give him certain important jobs to do. You see, Red Cloud was a leader because a man that can stand fearless in the heat of battle and calmly lead his people is a true warrior."

Everyone in the barn sat quietly as they thought about what Talks Right had said. In Indian ways it is not enough to just be good in battle, a true warrior cared about his people and put them first. A true warrior is also a spiritual man who recognizes that the Creator is in all things.

Talks Right seemed to be a little tired from the long journey, so Looks Long suggested that they take a break for awhile. They all agreed that the day was still young. Looks Long and Talks Right decided that they would fly off to find some lunch since the rain had finally stopped. The conversation once again turned to Little Feet and his new pups. Amy was all a flitter as she asked questions about the new babies. Little Feet could not hide the pride in his voice or his face. She sat next to Little Feet with her arm around his shoulder.

"I'm going to go in the house and bring us back some sandwiches." Lance rubbed his stomach and turned to the barn door. Just outside the door his blood froze. There was his father with a rifle in his hand. "Just be quiet son, that wolf next to Amy is a clean shot. If we startle him he may hurt her."

"Pa! No!" Lance screamed, "He's our friend."

With the sound of Lance's voice Little Feet leaped away from Amy but the shot was fired. Amy screamed as Little Feet fell to the ground. "No! No!" Tears flooded her face. Lance was in shock as he ran towards Little Feet, the sound of gunfire still echoing in his ears. Major Wheeling stood confused.

Kneeling by Little Feet, Lance began to cry. "Little Feet say something."

"I'm fine boy. The bullet missed me but I hit my head on that barn pole and I feel a little dazed." Little Feet looked up and saw Major Wheeling staring down at him with his mouth open wide. It was too late - Major Wheeling had heard Little Feet speak.

Amy and Lance stared up at Major Wheeling, not knowing what to do or say. Tears stained their faces. He knelt down next to Little Feet and placed his hand on Little Feet's back, still stunned from what had just took place. "Oh my god, it's true." Major Wheeling could not hide the anguish in his face. His heart felt as if were about to break.

"What's true, Pa?" Lance's mind was whirling. He had never seen his father look or act this way before.

"Years ago I was stationed at Fort Sill in the Oklahoma Territory. I met a lot of Indians from a lot of different tribes there. Many of the older ones told me that long before the white man came the animals would talk. They talked to the animals all the time since the animals had no language barrier and could speak all languages. They had a wonderful relationship with the animals. Then the animals saw the buffalo being slaughtered and almost disappear. They vowed to never talk again." Major Wheeling's voice was unsteady. "I thought it was just a story but its not – it's true."

Little Feet looked deep into Major Wheeling's eyes. "Yes, it's true and let the worry leave your face, you didn't hurt me. I'll be fine." Little Feet stood up still unsteady from the fall.

Major Wheeling looked at Lance and Amy, his mind was flooded with thought. He realized that this is why Lance had not been focused on his school work and why Amy and Lance kept whispering secrets to each other. Suddenly it all came clear to him that Amy wasn't there by chance she needed to live with them and not go to boarding school. Major Wheeling and his wife had talked about Amy living with them for some time. As if Little Feet could read his thoughts he quietly said, "She will learn more from us then at boarding school. She will also learn about who she is."

"I know that now." Major Wheeling looked towards the sky, his voice turned soft. "I guess this changes everything. I had my doubts in the past but not now. These kids can learn more from animals then they could ever imagine." Major Wheeling suddenly realized that he was talking out loud. He placed his hands on his son's shoulders. "Lance, I realize that you and Amy have had quite an adventure so far this summer, but I have the feeling the adventure has just begun. There is so much more for you to learn. What am I saying? There is so much more for me to learn as well."

"Are you going to tell Ma?" Lance wasn't sure how his mother would react.

"Not right now. We do need to talk about Amy staying with us and going to school with you. I don't know what all needs to be done but we will find out. If we have to your Ma can teach her here at the house. The main thing is this, Amy do you want to stay here with us? This can be your home from now on, but the decision is yours. I don't want you to live here if you don't think you would be happy. "

Amy was sitting next to Little Feet with her arms around his neck. Her tear stained face turned into a smile. Her heart was bursting with joy. A place that she could finally call home was a dream come true. "I feel like I belong here Uncle. I can learn about my heritage from the animals and maybe I will fit in better at Lance's school. Plus Auntie can teach me how to cook and sew and other things, you know, girl things. I will miss living with Pa though."

"Why would you miss me Amy?" No one had heard Andrew walk into the barn. "Can we live here Pa? I can go to school with Lance and Auntie can..."

Andrew interrupted, "Be a good Ma to you? Amy, I have been talking to your Aunt about this very thing for quite some time. That's the real reason I brought you out here." Andrew reached out and patted Little Feet on the head. No one was sure how long Andrew had been standing there listening but he showed no fear of Little Feet. "Your Ma use to talk to the animals." Andrew looked at Little Feet but seemed to be looking into the past, remembering his wife. "I kinda figured that what's been going on. Amy, things have been hard for us since your mother died yet I just didn't want to take your Aunt and Uncle up on their offer if you weren't going to be happy." Andrew looked at Major Wheeling with tears of happiness in his eyes. "Well brother in law I guess we better think about building that cabin you and I talked about."

Lance jumped straight up in the air "Yea!" Amy danced in circles and clapped her hands.

With all the excitement no one noticed Little Feet leave the barn. Little Feet's large paws never made a noise as he began to trot towards home. He had his own family to attend to and he had been gone long enough. Little Feet knew that family is the most important thing in life. Just as he entered the wood line he heard Looks Long and Talks Right call out to him from a large pine tree. Little Feet sat down under the branch they were perched on and looked up at them. "Well I have much to teach my new little ones and it seems like the two of you have much to teach your two little human ones as well."

Looks Long and Talks Right puffed out their feathers with pride. Looks Long cocked his pure white head sideways and looked down at Little Feet. "Yes, yes we will teach them well."

Talks Right nodded his head, "Time to go home." As they flew off you could still hear Talks Right Voice. His voice seemed to catch on the winds an echo through the trees.

The sun had completely come out and all the clouds had disappeared as Amy walked with her father back to the house. The rain had left everything smelling clean and fresh. In mid step she stopped and whispered to Lance. "Did you hear that?"

"Hear what?" Lance returned her quizzical look.

"I heard a voice in the wind saying time to go home." Amy's voice squeaked.

"You are home Amy." Mrs. Wheeling stood in the doorway with her arms open wide. "You are home.

RED CLOUD PICTURES

Photo by David F. Barry

"They made us many promises, more than I can remember.
But they kept but one – they promised to take our land and
they took it."

Red Cloud delegation. Left to right: Red Dog, Little Wound, John Bridgeman (interpreter), Red Cloud, American Horse, and Red Shirt. Oglala Sioux, before 1876.

Red Cloud (1822-1909)

"My sun is set. My day is done. Darkness is stealing over me. Before I lie down to rise no more, I will speak to my people.

Hear me, my friends, for it is not the time for me to tell you a lie. The Great Spirit made us, the Indians, and gave us this land we live in.He gave us the buffalo, the antelope, and the deer for food and clothing. We moved our hunting grounds from the Minnesota to the Platte and from the Mississippi to the great mountains. No one put bounds on us. We were free as the winds, and like the eagle, heard no man's commands.

I was born a Lakota and I shall die a Lakota."

AMERICAN INDIANS' GIFTS TO THE WORLD

A avocado, amaranth, asphalt

B buffalo, beaver pelts, beans

C canoe, corn, caucus, chocolate, cocoa, cotton, cashews, catfish, chilies, cayenne

D democracy, dyes, dogsleds

E ecology

F fertilizer, food preservation

G gum, guano deposits, grits, gold

H hammock, hominy, hickory nut, herbs

I impeachment, ipecac

J jerky, Jerusalem artichoke

K kidney beans, kayaks

L libraries, long pants, llamas

M milpa, moccasins, manioc, medicines

N nuts, names (half the states names of USA)

O oranges

P potatoes, pumpkins, peanuts, popcorn, pineapple, passenger pigeon, pear cactus, peppers, pecan, paprika

Q quinine

R rubber

S squash, silver, sisal, sunflowers, sweet potatoes, succotash

T turkey, tapioca pudding, tomatoes, tobacco, tar

U United States Constitution – influenced by the Iroquois

V vanilla

W wild rice, witch hazel

X xylophone

Y yams

Z zero, zucchini

FOOD OF THE AMERICAN INDIANS

Nuts
Acorns
Beechnuts
Butternuts
Coffee Tree Seeds
Hazel Nuts
Hickory Nuts
Peanuts
Pecans
Pinon Nuts
Walnuts

Vegetables
Artichokes
Beans
Gourds
Corn (maize)
Potatoes
Pumpkins
Squash
Sunflower Seeds
Tomatoes
Wild Rice
Mushrooms
Turnips
Pigweed Seeds
Greens
When Corn, Potatoes, Beans
  (The Three Sisters) were
  introduced to Europe ended

the almost annual famines that
constantly plagued the White
Man. *(See Indian Givers –
Weatherford, J.)*
The tomato, mushrooms and
various herbs significantly
enhanced his culinary tastes.
*(See Indian Givers – Weather-
ford, J.)*

Flowers
Adders tongue
Cattails
Honey Locust Seeds
Nayuapple
Pigweed Seeds
Primrose
Solomons Seal
Herbs
Water Lily

Wild Berries
Blackberries
Cranberries
Elderberries
Gooseberries
Hackberries
Haws
Huckleberries
Raspberries
Strawberries

Wild Fruit
Cherries
Crabapples
Currants
Grapes
Maple Sugar
Melons
PawPaws
Persimmons
Plums

Meat
Antelope
Bear
Beaver
Elk
Buffalo
Deer
Rabbit
Moose
Muskrat
Opossum
Raccoon
Squirrel

Fowl
Various Small Birds
Bird eggs
Wild Duck
Turkeys

Fish
Abalone
Clams
Crayfish
Crabs
Frogs
Oysters
Snails
Turtles
Various Fish from lakes
    and streams

LAKOTA DICTIONARY

This is a list of commonly used words, some of which may be heard in ceremony or associated with prayer. Spelling of most words is not consistent; the list below is usually spelled phonetically. Some variation in accent exists among the Sioux tribes. Chan and chun are examples; chanupa or chunupa for pipe. Definition of horse for example varies; ṣunka wakan or tah ṣunka wakan. Often the n is barely heard at the end of a syllable. Wakan Tanka sounds like Wah kahhn Tahn kah. A smaller font n will be used for this expression since this is practical and a capability of the modern word processor.

C̲	ch as in chain	C	C as in cold
H̲	hk as in hahkk		
K̲	gutteral sound as in kh	K	K as in kite
S̲	sh as in Shell	S	S as in sit
T̲	gutteral sound as in tkh	T	T as in tie

* * * *

LAKOTA SIOUX WORDS

Pronunciations are phonetic where necessary to better understand.

again ak̲e (ah khay)
all of you help me omakiya po
all powers wowas ake iyuha
All things on earth Maka Sitomni (mah kha see toe mnee)
alone isna (ee shnah)
ancestor, relative hunka (hoon kah)

awakening to wisdom woksapa kiwani (woke sah pah kee wan nee)

awakening kiwan (kee wah nee)

baby hokshi cala

bad, wrong, not good sica (she cha)

beads hokomi

big storm, strong north wind wahziya ahtah

Black Elk Heh haka Sapa

Black Hills Paha Sapa (pa ha sa pa)

blonde haired hinze (hin zhee)

boy hoksila (hoke she la)

Buffalo Calf Woman Pte cinchala Ska Wakan Winan (pta heen cha la ska wa kan we ahn)

buffalo cow pte (ptay)

call or cry out hoyeya (ho yay ya)

camp police, marshall akicita (ah khee chee tah), a representative or messenger of a supernatural being or power

center cokato (cho kah to), cokato center

ceremony wakicaga

ceremony wakan wicohan (weechohan)

Ceremony of Clown Making heyoka kaga

chief, leader itancan (ee tahn chan)

child hoksi (hoke shee)

children of the earth wakanyeja makah

circle, camp circle hocokan (ho cho kan), sacred altar in a ritual

clear bleaza

clown or a contrary heyoka (hee yoh kah), one who makes you laugh; those who do things backwards and wear shabby clothes; one who has dreamed of thunder and lightning and believes he should act in an unnatural or contrary manner

come, follow closely hakamya upo (hah kahm yah you po)
cottonwood tree waga chun
crying for a vision hanblecheya (han bleay chee ah)

dawn light anpo
drum cancega (chan chega)

Earth Maka (mah kha)
east wiyoheyapa (wee yo he yah pa), rising dawn
east power wiyoheyapata ouye, rising dawn of the east direction
exclamation of acknowledgement ah ho
extended family tiyospaye (tee yo spi yeh)
eye ista (ish tah)

Father Sky Mahpiyah Ate (Mak pi yah Ah tay)
Father Sun Wiyo Ate (wee yo ah teh)
Feather wiyaka (we ya kah)
fire peta (pay tah)
flower wanaca (wah nah cha), Look at me. Look at me!
flying owankinye (oh wan keen yea)
four directions, four winds tate topa (tah teay toe pah)
four leggeds hutopah
friend kola (koe lah)
future tokata (toe ka tah)
future generations tokata wicocage

Give Away ceremony oudu ha (o dtu ha)
go kigli
good looking, handsome wanyanke waste
            (ah wahn yahn kay wah stay)
good waste (wash tay)
good fortune, good luck oglu wahste

Great Spirit, Great Mystery Wakan Tanka
(Wah kahhn Tahn kah)
grow icaga (ee ca ga) (ee ca ga)

hair roach pay sha
happy, pleasant wihahaya (win ha ha yah)
hau! interjection of affirmation
heh expression at end of sentence
heart cante (chanh tay)
heavy rainfall minne ahtah, much rain
hello hau (houw)
help me omakiya (o ma kee ya)
heyoka wachipi, clown at dances; funny dancer at dances
high sun wiyo ichoni, sun at its height is giving life
holy man wichasha wakan
holy woman winan wakan (wee ahn wah kahn)
holy, sacred wakan (wah kahn)
hoop cangleska (chan gleas kha)

I am not afraid hoka (hoke ah)
I give cicu (chee choo)
Indian way Lakol wicohan
I pray (chey wa key ya cewakiya)
it is so; amen hecitu (hehche too)

Lakota (lah koe tah), Allies, friends, name for Western,
Teton Sioux
life giving rains wichoni (wee cho nee minn ee)
lightning wakinyan
listen anagoptan (a nagho p' tan)
lo (low), expression at end of sentence. 'I am listening to you.'
look itunwa (ee toon wah)
looking, watching ahitunwan (a he toon wan)

love, of the heart c̲anhiya (chan hin yan)
loving couple c̲antkiya (chan teh kee ya)

making of Relatives Ceremony Hunkapi
man wichasha (wee cha sha)
medicine pejuta (pay zjhoo tah)
medicine man pejuta wichasha (pay zjhoo tah we cha sha)
medicine woman pejuta winan (pay zjhoo tah we ahn)
misun (mee soon), man's term for younger brother
Moon hanwi (sacred term hanwe-kan)
moon hanhepi wi hanheaypi
Morning Star anpo wicahpi (ahn poh wee chak peh)
Mother Earth Ina Maka (ee nah mah kah)
my miye (mee yea)
mystic warrior wichasta ohuze (o hoo zhea)

nation, tribe oyate (oh yah tay)
no hiya
north waziya (wah zee yah)
now ho wana (ho wah nah)

observe everything as you walk ak̲ita mani yo
        (ah kee tah mah nee yo)
observer ahbleza (ah blay zah)
offerings wanunyanp

peace pipe c̲anupa (chan oon pah or chun oo pah)
personal charm wotawe (woe tah weh), broader term
        for personal stone
personal stone wotai (woe tie), personal stone that has
        appeared to you, you carry it at times, your personal
        gift from Wakan Tanka
power of the north waziya ouye (prayer for the north)

pray cekiya (chey key ya) or chey key yah yea.
protect, to look over awanyanka (ah wahn yahn ka)

red pipe canupa lutah
red stone inyansa (in yahn shah)
red willow bark tobacco cansasa (chan sha sha)
Remember minksuyan (mink sue yan)
road, way, path canku (chan koo)
rock, stone inyan (in yahn)

sacred hoop cangleska wakan (chan gleas kha wah kan)
Sacred Pipe Canupa Wakan
sage, sacred herb of the north peju ota (pay zjhoo o tah)
Salt miniskuya (minn ee sku ee ya)
say iya (ee ya)
see wayaka see (wan yan ka)
send a voice, expression of assent hoye (ho yay)
shine, glisten wiyakpa
sing now wana olowanpi
singing in praise alowanpi (a lo wan pee)
Six powers of the Universe Shakopeh Ouye
sky, clouds mahpiya (mak pi yah)
sleep istima (ee shtee mah)
song olowan (oh low wan)
south itokaga (ee toe ka gha)
speak kihowaya (ke ho wa ya)
spider iktomi (unk to mee or, ee kto mee), the tricky spider
    fellow in Sioux stories, trickster or jokester
spirit wanagi (wah nah gee, wah nah ghee)
spirit, ghosts nagi (nah ghee or nah zhee)
spirit calling ceremony yuwipi (yoo wee pee), they tie him up
star wicahpi (wi chak pi)
sugar canhanpi (chan han pee)
sun anpetu wi

Sun Dance Ceremony wiwanyag wachipi
Sun anpetu wi (ahn pay too wee)
sun, moon wi (wee)
sweat lodge ceremony inipi (ee nee pee)
sweat lodge initi (ee nee tee)

thank you pilamiya (pee lam ay ah, pee lam ee yah)
thank you very much pilamaya aloh or yelo
the medicine world pejuta makah wakan
the winged people zintkala oyate (zint kha la o yah teh)
these lena these (ley nah)
this le (ley)
those hina (hee na)
thunder wakinyan hotonpi
thunder beings wakinyan tanka
thunder hawk wakinyan cetan (wah keen yan che tan)
to speak iyaya
to tell dreams and visions hanbloglagia (hahn blo glah gee ah)
tobacco kinnic kinnick (kin nic kinn nic)
tobacco canli (chan lee)
tobacco offering canli wapahte (chan lee wah pahk teh)
tree canpaza (chan pah zah), old term for tree
two leggeds hununpa

very good lelah wah ste (lee lah wah ste)
vision quest hanblecheyapi

wait ahpe (ah pay)
warrior wichasta warrior (wee cha stah)
Water mini water (minn ee)
We are all related Mitakuye Oyasin (me ta koo yea oh ya seen),
      We are related to all things; We are all related; We are all
      relatives

west wiyopeyata (wee yo peh yah ta), the sun is setting in the direction of west

west power; power of the setting sun wiyopeyata ouye

white man washichu (wah she chu), literally, he reaches for all things

Wind tate (tah teay)

winged, bird huya (khoo yah)

wisdom woksapa (woke sah pah)

woman winan (wee ahn)

wood can (chanh), tree, wood; prefix for things made of or related to wood

ANIMALS

animals wamakaskan (wah mah kha skan), Animal World

antelope heton cik'ala

badger hoka

bat hupakiglake

bear mato (mah toe)

bear, grizzly waonze

bear, black mato sapa

bear, brown mato hi

bear, polar mato ska

beaver capa (cha pah)

bobcat igmu sinteksa

buffalo, (bull) tatanka

buffalo, (cow) pte

calf ptehincala

cat igmu

coyote masleca, sunkmanitu

deer tahca

deer, female tahca winyela

deer, (fawn) tingleska

dog sunka

elk, (bull) heha<u>k</u>a
elk, (cow) unpan
ferret itopta sapa, taunkasa
fox <u>s</u>un<u>g</u>ila, to<u>k</u>ala
frog wa<u>s</u>'in, gnaska
gopher itgnila, wahinheya
horse <u>s</u>uun<u>k</u>awakan, holy dog (horse), <u>T</u>ah<u>sh</u>uunkawakan, very
    large dog holy (horse) "A human can ride this large dog. It
    must be holy." Expression when Sioux first saw a horse.
jackal mayasle
lizard agleska
lion igmu <u>t</u>an<u>k</u>a
marten wah'ank<u>sic</u>a
mule sonsonla
mink iku<u>s</u>an
mouse (h)itun<u>k</u>ala
muskrat sinkpe
otter ptan
porcupine pahin
prairie dog pispiza
rabbit mastin<u>c</u>a
raccoon wica, wi<u>c</u>iteglega
skunk maka
squirrel het<u>k</u>ala, zi<u>c</u>a (red)
wolf <u>s</u>unkmanitu tan<u>k</u>a

REPTILES AND FISH

clam tuki
fish ho ghan
leech tusla
minnow hogan<u>s</u>anla
orca or porpoise ho ghan wakan, It thinks like a human, is
    highly intelligent, therefore must be holy (Wakan).

rattlesnake sintehla
snail mniwamnuh'a
snake zuzeca (zoo zeh cha)
tadpole hona itkala
toad mapih'a
turtle ke or keya (Key yah)
turtle, sand patka sa
turtle, snapping keya samna
water snake mni zuzeca
whale hogan tanka

BIRDS

birds Zintkala (Zint kah lah), Flying Ones
blackbird wablosa
bluebird zintkato (zint kha toe)
buzzard hecan
chickadee skipipi
cowbird pteyahpa
crane, white pehanska
crow kangi (kahn zhee)
dove, morning wakinyela
duck magaksica
eagle wanbli (wahn blee)
goose maga (mah gah)
grouse cansiyo
gull wicatankala
hawk cetan (che tahn)
hawk, night cetan, pisko
heron hokagica
hummingbird tanagila
jay zintkatogleglega
killdeer pehincicila
kingbird wasnasnaheca

lark   istanica tanka
loon   bleza
magpie   halhate, unkcekiha
meadowlark   winapinla, jialepa
mud hen (duck)   siyaka
oriole   skeluta
owl   hinhan
prairie chicken   siyoka
quail   siyo cik'ala
raven   kangi ta
robin   sisoka
sparrow   ihuhaotila
swallow   hupucansakala
swan   magaska
thrush   caguguyasa
turkey   wagleksun
woodcock   kankeca
wood duck   skiska
woodpecker   wagnuka
wren   canheyala

NUMBERS

One   Wanji
Two   Núnpa
Three   Yámni
Four   Tópa
Five   Záptan
Six   Shakpeh
Seven   Shaklogan
Eight   Shakgowin
Nine   Numchinka
Ten   wanji nunpah

COLORS - FOUR DIRECTIONS

yellow zi zi (zhee zhee)
red sa (sha)
black sapa (sah pah)
white ska

RELATIVES

Mother Ina (ee nah)
Father ahte (ah tay)
Grandfather Tankashilah (taunk ah she lah)
Grandmother Unci
Sister hakata
Brother tiblo
Niece tojan
Nephew tunska
Uncle Leksi (lake she)
Cousin tahansi, male hankasi, female
Friend kola
Tribal relatives Oyate (Oh yah teah), The People, Tribe, Nation